What readers are saying...

"Follows a young boy as he embarks on a magical journey to Candy Ville. During his travels, he discovers how being a good and respectful person can really pay off."
— **Foreword Reviews**

"Dr. Gerry Haller's picture book story, Will's Adventure to the Candy Mountain, is an entertaining story for young readers.... The story is sweet (not candy sweet) and simple, but the message is clear: life is full of sweet offerings, but friendship and kindness are more important than sweet treats. One has to always be courteous. Beautifully told and presented."
— **Emily-Jane Hills Orford, Readers' Favorite**

"Gerry Haller's gentle tale is inspired by stories she told to her grandson. Her vivid descriptions of Candy Mountain's "gumdrops of many colors, candy canes, gingerbread men and women all over the branches of the tree" will charm young readers. Cho's colorful, dreamy paintings of giant lollipop trees and ice cream–coated mountaintops complement the story. Adults will appreciate that the book celebrates and rewards good behavior.... Full of wonder but lacking tension, the narrative is a pleasant read-aloud. Placid and relaxing, Will's ramble through Candy Mountain is sure to inspire sweet dreams. This relaxing journey through a land of treats is a pleasant low-key bedtime story for young children."
— **BookLife Review**

"A story that uses timely topics, up-to-date story concepts, and creates an integration of the child and the reader to go on a journey together. The story takes us on an adventure that lightens our senses with the words and beautiful artwork. A story that creates a new experience with magic, dreams, and wonderment. To learn compassion from a child's point of view also allows the parent, grandparent, or reader to also explore how they too can become more compassionate. What a wonderful engagement of souls."
— **Dr. Jeanette Gallagher, ND Blogspot Radio**

"The full-page illustrations by YM Cho are colorful and fun. Children will love looking at the pages. I enjoyed counting the numerous kinds of candies and saw all my favorites pictured there. My favorite things were the lessons the story cleverly taught. When Will gets on the train, he immediately finds another boy, named Quinn, sitting alone. Will introduces himself, and the pair become new friends. The children are well-mannered and courteous, always saying please and thanking the gingerbread people for their help. The train conductor tells the children they must return to the train when it blows its whistle. Will and Quinn rush back from their adventures, not wanting to be late. Also, only good children are allowed to pass through Candy Mountain's gate. Friendship, politeness, punctuality, and exemplary behavior are all valuable lessons for children to learn."
    — **OnlineBookClub.org**

"Gifted educator and author Dr. Gerry Haller presents a delicious and wholesome fantasy story that will touch the hearts of readers of all ages in her new children's picture book Will's Adventure to the Candy Mountain. More than just a sweet experience, the entertaining story also instills the importance of being a good and kind person, as well as the benefits that can be gained with it."
    — **Motherhood-Moment.blogspot.com, Book Nook**

"Readers will be asking for seconds (of reading the book again, that is) after they finish this charming story and will be reminded that good things come to those who are respectful and considerate."
    — **Groovin Moms**

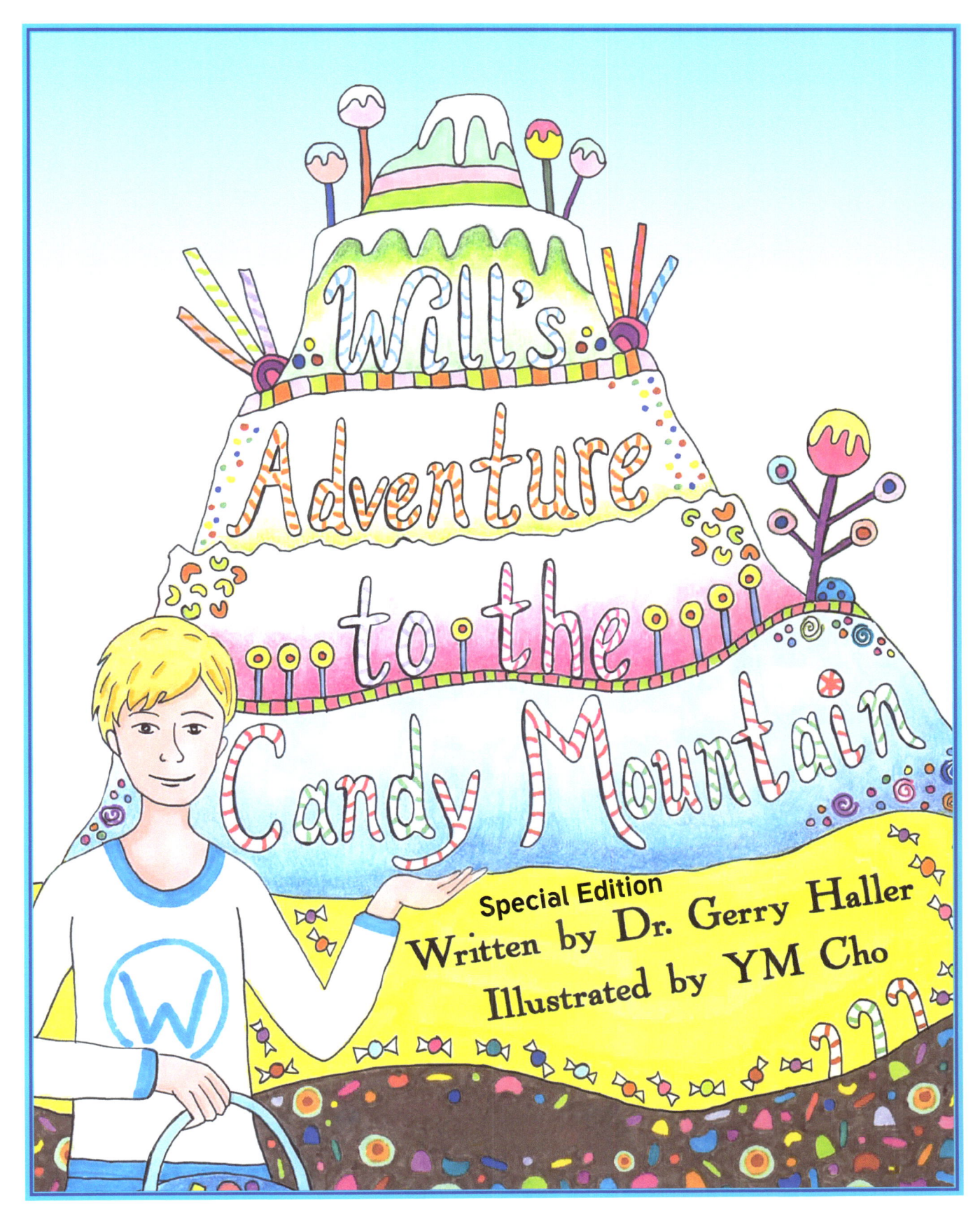

ISBN 978-1-967362-21-9 (paperback)
ISBN 978-1-967362-12-7 (hardcover)
ISBN 978-1-967362-11-0 (ebook)

Copyright © 2025 by Gerry Haller

All rights reserved. No part of this publication may be reproduced, distributed, or transmitted in any form or by any means, including photocopying, recording, or other electronic or mechanical methods without the prior written permission of the publisher.

Printed in the United States of America

DEDICATION

To my grandson Will who felt everyone should hear this story.
— Grandma

Will's grandmother tucked him and his brothers into bed every Saturday night. She loved telling the story of Candy Mountain, a place she visited as a child. Only exceptionally good children could pass through its gates. Each time she told the tale, Will vividly imagined her words.

Tonight, Will listened, excitement bubbling as she spoke. When the story ended, he asked, "Grandma, please lie down with me."

She snuggled close and hugged him until he fell asleep.

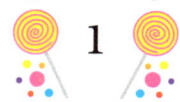

A hand shook Will awake. "Time to go," said a voice. Will opened his eyes to see a thin woman with curly black hair and a conductor's hat.

"Go where?" he asked.

"To Candy Mountain!" she replied.

Will jumped up, put on his slippers, and followed the conductor to the train, amazed he was heading to Candy Mountain.

Will couldn't believe his eyes—a huge steam engine with four passenger cars waited at the end of his street.

The train was magical: a white car with gumdrops, a green car with candy corn, a red car with gingerbread men, and a blue car with candy canes.

The conductor helped Will board the gingerbread car, where many children sat, talking and looking out the window.

Will sat beside a boy sitting alone.

"Hi, I'm Will. What's your name?" he asked.

"Quinn," the boy replied.

The train began to move. Will and Quinn watched as the city's sparkling lights twinkled in the dark. Soon, the train left the city behind.

Will gazed at the bright full moon, its silver light illuminating homes, streets, and cars.

"Everything looks beautiful in the moonlight," he said.

"It's amazing," Quinn replied.

As they entered the wilderness, tall trees appeared.

"What are those shiny circles in the trees?" Quinn asked.

"Maybe owls' eyes," Will replied.

Next, they passed lush farmland with animals out at night. "Look, cattle eating grass!" said Will.

"And sheep and pigs," Quinn added.

Mostly, there were cornfields.

    The train sped up, and the view outside changed. It climbed a mountain, circled back down, and crossed flat land. They passed a valley with charming houses. Then the train went higher and higher into the mountain.

"Will we be there soon?" asked Will.

"I hope so," said Quinn.

The train kept going until Will saw bright lights ahead. They were nearing a train station.

It looked like a sparkling white gingerbread house with colorful sprinkles on the roof. The train slowed down.

"I can read the sign!" Will said. "It says Candy Ville."

On the platform, he saw colorful, child-sized baskets.

The conductor entered and said, "We're here in the land of candy and fun! Pick a basket for your treats — any color you like. But remember, when the train blows its horn, hurry back, or it will leave!"

The children squealed and laughed as they got off the train.

"Come with me, Quinn," Will said. "I need a friend for this adventure."

"Me too," Quinn agreed, and they jumped off the train together.

Will couldn't believe his eyes. The station was made of gingerbread and candy. Baskets sat on the platform in front of it.

"I'm taking a blue basket. It's my favorite color," said Will.

"I want a purple one," said Quinn, grabbing a purple basket.

They walked to the gate and saw the mountain sparkling with every color. The top was white like snow.

The gate sparkled with all kinds of candy—gumdrops, gummy bears, marshmallows, candy canes, licorice, and jellybeans.

The conductor opened the gate and said, "Welcome to Candy Mountain! Only good children can enter. This is your reward for being good."

The children ran in all directions. Will spotted a tall tree in the distance.

"Quinn, look at that tree! Let's go there first," said Will.

"OK," Quinn replied.

While the others ran to Candy Mountain, Will and Quinn headed toward the tree.

When they arrived, they saw it was very tall with candy hanging from its branches—gumdrops, candy canes, and gingerbread figures.

Will wondered how they could reach the candy. Then he noticed a white sign with black letters next to the tree. It said, *"If you need help, call a Gingerbread Man."*

A gingerbread man jumped out from behind the tree. "Do you need my help?" he asked.

"Yes, please," said Will. "How do we get the candy?"

"I'll shake the branches, and the candy will fall," answered the gingerbread man.

He climbed into the tree and shook the branches. Candy fell to the ground, and the boys quickly filled their baskets.

Candy fell to the ground, and the boys quickly filled their baskets.

"This was a great idea," said Will. "But we should head to Candy Mountain now."

"Look, there it is!" Will pointed.

After a long walk, Will and Quinn reached the foot of Candy Mountain.

It stood tall and majestic, glowing with bright colors in the morning sun. Candy was everywhere!

"This is going to be an adventure," said Will. "Are you ready?"

"I can't wait!" answered Quinn.

They started up the mountain and found chocolate. They picked a chocolate cat and some chocolate drops.

As they climbed higher, they spotted red licorice and added it to their baskets.

They also picked lemon slices, sugary orange slices, jellybeans, and gummy bears in every color. Their baskets were getting full, and so were they.

"Let's go," said Will. "We need to reach the top of the mountain."

Soon, they reached the top of Candy Mountain, and their baskets were heavy. They were tired but amazed.

"Look, Will," said Quinn. "You can see forever!"

From the top, they could see a lake, a river with a bridge, and a small village. There was so much to explore!

Will touched the snow and said, "Oh my! This doesn't feel like snow." He tasted it and was surprised—it was ice cream!

Quinn tasted it too. "Yum! How can we carry it?"

Will found paper cups and spoons. They scooped ice cream into the cups and headed down the mountain toward the lake.

When they got there, they saw a sign that said "The Root Beer Lake" and a gingerbread girl by a tree.

"Want a cup?" she asked.

"Yes, thank you," the boys said, taking cups from her.

They scooped root beer from the lake and poured it over ice cream to make root beer floats. Then, they sat by the lake to enjoy their treat.

"That was so good!" said Will.

Now it was time to go to the river. What adventure would they find there? Everything so far was amazing!

Will saw a tree near the river. As he got closer, he saw a gingerbread girl standing by it.

"Welcome to the Chocolate River," she said. "Would you like an ice cream sundae?"

"Yes!" the boys said.

They took ice cream from the gingerbread girl, added chocolate from the river, and topped it with whipped cream and a cherry.

The boys sat under the tree with their sundaes.

"This is so good," said Quinn. "I wonder if I'll have room for more?"

Will looked at the bridge, wondering what might be on the other side. He stood up and said, "Quinn, I think we have another adventure waiting."

Quinn nodded. "I think you're right."

The boys crossed the bridge, ready for a new adventure.

    They followed the path to the Snow People Village. It was the most beautiful place they had ever seen. The village had one street running through the middle.

The houses were made of gingerbread, each decorated with colorful frosting and candy. Every house looked unique with its own design.

Snow people were busy all over the village.

The snow women wore colorful knitted hats with flowers on the brim and scarves around their necks. Their faces were made of candy.

The snowmen wore candy top hats and colorful scarves. Their faces and buttons were made of candy.

The snow children dressed just like the adults.

Will saw a factory with a store and a sign that said "Bakery."

"Hey, Quinn, want to check out the Bakery?" Will asked.

"Yes, the factory looks interesting. I want to see what's happening there," Quinn answered.

So, the boys went down the street to explore.

When the boys entered the store, the snow people smiled at them. Will saw candy, cookies, and gingerbread men with frosting in the display cases. The factory was to the left, where snow people were happily working.

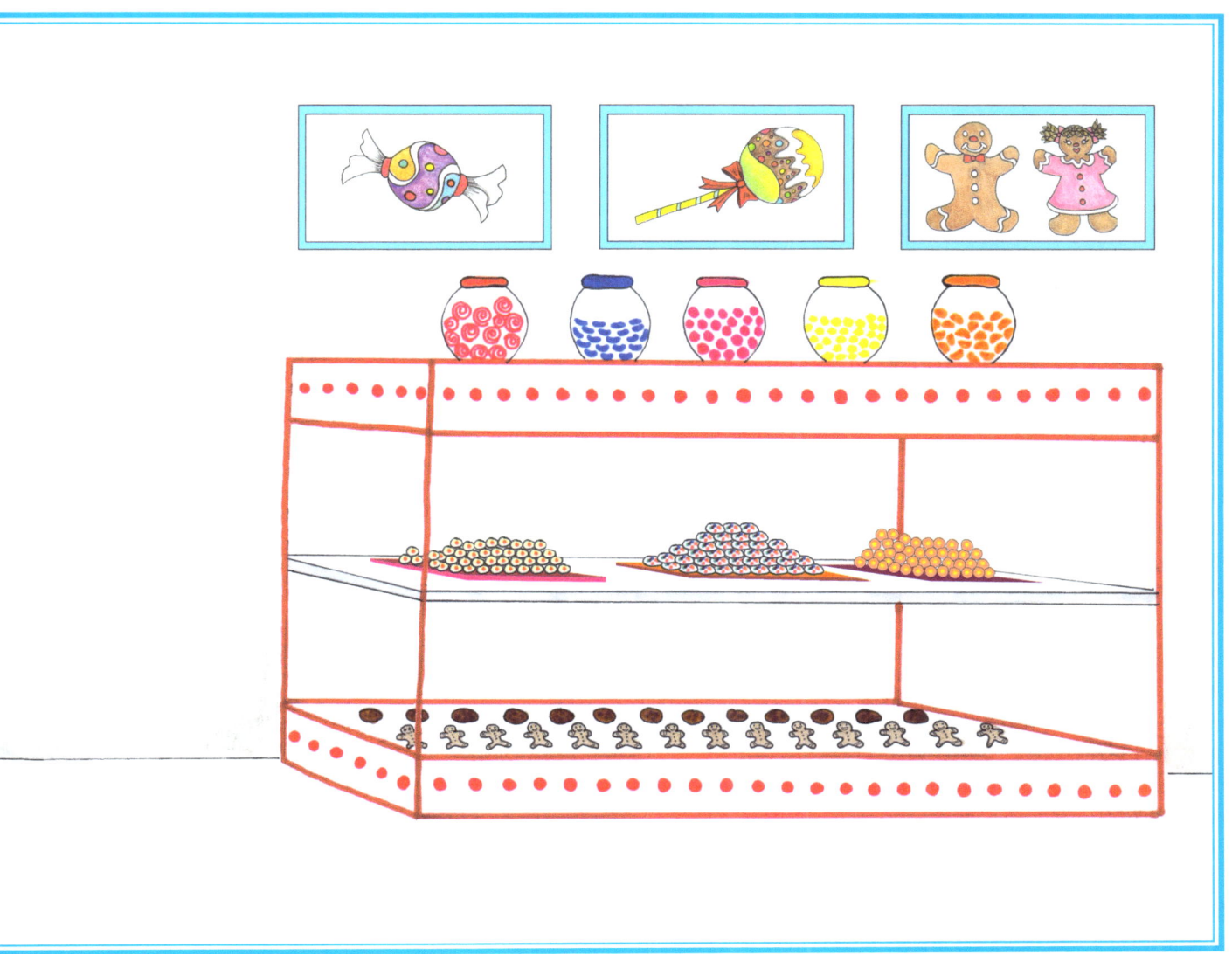

    The factory smelled amazing. Besides the cookies, everything looked like candy from Candy Mountain. Will wondered, *Did everyone work together to make this adventure so special?*

A snow lady asked if they wanted anything for their baskets. Will set his basket down and looked at the display case. He already had a lot, but said, "I'd like the cookie with the cherry in the middle."

The snow lady took the cookie from the display and handed it to him.

Will took a bite of the cookie and smiled. "This is delicious! Thank you for being so kind," he said.

Quinn picked a cookie with a chocolate drop in the middle. He took a bite and said, "Yummy, yummy in my tummy," then giggled.

The boys smiled and waved goodbye as they left.

Will noticed it was getting late. "Hey, Quinn, we'd better hurry!" The boys ran down the street, along the path, and over the bridge. Suddenly, they heard the train's horn.

"Oh no!" Will shouted. "We need to run faster!"

    Will and Quinn sprinted toward the train as fast as they could. Will wondered, *If we miss the train, how will we get home?* They kept running.

Finally, they saw the exit sign from Candy Mountain and ran faster. Will's heart was racing. Would they make it on time? He saw the train was still at the station. The boys ran through the exit sign just as they heard, "All aboard!"

"Wait! Wait! We're coming!" Will shouted. Could the conductor hear him?

"Wait! Wait!" both boys yelled. The train tooted as they reached the conductor.

"I'm here," said Will.

"I'm here too," added Quinn.

"Good to see you both. Did you have a good time?" asked the conductor.

"We had an amazing adventure! I'll never forget it," Will replied as he and Quinn jumped onto the train.

The conductor waved her lantern to the engineer, and the train jolted forward, bumping as it went.

Will looked for a double seat in the gumdrop car but couldn't find one. They moved to the candy corn car, but no seats there either. Finally, he found two seats together in the candy cane car.

Will and Quinn flopped into their seats, tired from all they had seen and done.

"It was an adventure I'll never forget," said Will.

"Oh no! Quinn, I left my candy basket at the bakery," said Will. "I forgot it on the floor."

"I'm sorry, Will. There's nothing we can do now. Want to share mine?" asked Quinn.

"That's okay, Quinn. Thanks for being so kind. I wish I could always know you," said Will.

Will thought about their adventure.

"You know, Quinn, everything was so much fun. At least I have the memories. I'll never forget them," said Will.

"Neither will I," said Quinn.

The train rocked, and Will, tired from the excitement, slowly fell asleep.

When Will woke up, he was in his bed under the covers.

How did I get here? he wondered.

He sat up, surprised. What an amazing night! He looked around and found his basket at the foot of the bed. How could that be? He had left it at the bakery.

Will grabbed his basket and ran down the hall.

"Grandmother! Grandmother!" he shouted, jumping onto her bed.

"You won't believe it! I went to Candy Mountain last night. It was amazing!" said Will.

"I'm so happy for you!" said Grandmother. "Tell me all about it. It sounds like a wonderful adventure!"

Will took a deep breath and began his story.

Questions & Activities

Will and Quinn went to the Candy Mountain. What was your favorite part of the story?

How do you think the conductor got into Will's room?

Was it all a dream? Or did it really happen? How do you know?

How did Will and Quinn get to the Candy Mountain? Have you ever taken a trip and traveled that way? Where did you go? Draw a picture of you and your friend or family taking a trip.

Will met Quinn along the way. If you went to a fun special place, who would you take with you? Why?

If you went to the Candy Mountain, what kinds of candy would you collect? How many kinds of candy in the story can you name? What are your favorites? Draw a picture of YOUR special Candy Mountain.

What color basket would you pick? How did you feel when Will realized he didn't have his basket? Would you have shared your candy? Why or why not? Did Will get his basket back? What did that tell you?

What were the snow people doing in the village? What were they wearing? And how did the gingerbread girl help Will and Quinn?

In the book, what did Will think about what was going on in the factory? What were the snow people doing? Why?

Will went to the Candy Mountain because he had been very good. What do you do around the house or with your friends to help out? What do your parents, grandparents, or friends say to you when you have done something good for them?

If you could have a wish to go to a special place, where would it be? Is it a real place or an imaginary place? Draw a picture to show what it is like there. Or tell a story about how you got there and what you did.

There was one thing the children were supposed to do when they heard the horn. What was that? Did Will and Quinn do it? Then what happened?

At the end of the story, where was Will? How did he get there? Where was his basket? How did it get there?

ABOUT THE AUTHOR

Dr. Gerry Haller is an accomplished educator. She has received many awards for being outstanding in teaching, curriculum, and administrative fields, including being recognized by the Carnegie Foundation for her teaching in the inner city of Chicago and receiving the Phi Delta Kappa Award for being the Outstanding Principal of the Year.

ABOUT THE ILLUSTRATOR

YM Cho is an award-winning artist and designer. She earned a BFA degree from the School of the Art Institute of Chicago, where she studied visual communications and fashion illustration. YM has won numerous art and design competitions, including the 2017 Leavenworth Oktoberfest Logo Design, the 2017 Navy Air Force Half Marathon shirt design, the 2019 Seward Silver Salmon Derby Logo Design, the 93rd Running Mount Marathon Logo Design, the 2022 Tumbleweed Music Festival Logo Design, and the 2025 Alaska's Women Gold Nugget Triathlon logo Design. www.ymchoartdesign.com.

www.ingramcontent.com/pod-product-compliance
Lightning Source LLC
LaVergne TN
LVHW070450080526
838202LV00035B/2794